Seduced by the Snowman

Seduced by the Snowman

Addison Kane

Amy-
thanks for the ~inspiration~
and the comic

It was four days before Christmas and, because I was forever a terrible procrastinator, I still had shopping to do.

Like, *a lot* of shopping. So far, I'd only bought a pair of earrings for my grandma and a box of treats for her diabetic poodle.

Wait, can her poodle even have *treats? Crap, maybe I should've gotten the thing a toy instead. Why am I even worried about getting a gift for a dog?*

At least I didn't seem to be the only dilly-dallier, though. My friend - and neighbor - Candice and I were attempting to battle our way through a jolly crowd of holiday shoppers just as last-minute as I was. Our small town's main thoroughfare was *packed* and we couldn't do much more than literally squeeze our way between the overwhelming press of bodies.

"Oh, wow, look at *that*," there was a low whistle and I spun to see the back of Candice's blonde head as she simultaneously admired a man's backside and tried not to spill hot cider on herself. She turned back around a moment later, grinning a little madly to herself, "that was *nice*."

"Real subtle," I smirked.

She wheezed, "but did you *see*?" And then began to fan herself dramatically. "Miss Isobel, I do believe I may swoon."

I had indeed seen and my shoulder lifted with my indifference. "Meh."

She straightened, aghast, "whattaya mean, '*meh*'?"

"I mean *meh*." It was true, the man had been pretty damn attractive, but nothing inside me had screamed, *I wonder what he'd look like without those jeans on.*

"What is *up with you, Scrooge*?" Candice poked me in the chest with a roll of metallic wrapping paper. "I'm starting to feel like I've lost my partner in crime over here."

My eyes found the concerned crinkle of her forehead. "I don't wanna talk about it. It's stupid," I sighed. "Excuse me," I muttered to the woman in front of us as we elbowed our way past her and her avalanche of shopping bags.

Candice's interest was piqued and I watched her lift one delicately plucked eyebrow, "but there's something to talk about?"

"Cee, this is not really the best place," my arms went as wide as they could, reminding her just how many people were skating along the icy sidewalks beside us.

Her dark eyes rolled, "*fine.* I'll drag it out of you later, then."

My lips pursed, "can't wait." I pulled a crumpled sheet of notebook paper from my coat pocket and squinted down at the chaotic handwriting.

Candice tried to read it over my shoulder. "How many people do you have left on there?"

I scrubbed a gloved hand over my face wearily, "eleven?"

"Jesus, Isobel," she sputtered, "if I'd have known you were this far behind, I would *not* have agreed to come out with you."

My lips twitched into a small smile, "yes, you would've."

"Yeah," she took a sip of her drink, hissing when she found it was *still* too hot, "but only because your panic amuses me."

My eyes narrowed, "wow, thanks."

"Okay, quite being a time-waster, who's next?"

"My cousin's boys," I answered.

"How many of them does she have now?"

"Four."

"Wait, did she have *another* one?"

I nodded, "in May."

Her tongue clicked against the roof of her mouth. *"Damn.* That's a lot of testosterone in one house."

"Time-waster."

"Well," she shrugged, "I don't know anything about little boys."

"Yeah, neither do I." We stared at each other for a full minute. "I could get all the big ones some of those foam dart guns?"

"That sounds like a *fucking* good time," Candice cawed. A middle-aged woman scowled in our direction, her nose wrinkled with disdain. "Dart guns! Let's go!"

Two more hot ciders later, Candice and I were hobbling down a much less crowded sidewalk in the direction of our apartment building.

"Man, we should've waited for your car to get out of the shop before we did this," she huffed, hiking her bags up once again.

"But I don't know when that's going to *be*," I sighed. "They said they had to order a part and, since it's the holidays, everything is backed up."

Candice growled her displeasure.

"Y'know, *you* could've offered to drive."

"I could've, yes," she sulked, dragging her feet along beside me, "but it never occurred to me how much this would *suck*."

I could only laugh.

"Hey," Candice wiggled her gloved fingers at the roughly hewn path right beside the sidewalk, "you wanna take the shortcut home?"

I nodded, already stepping off the concrete and into the small grove of pine trees. The leather of my boots sank into fluffy, fresh powder and Candice followed along behind, carefully tiptoeing inside the tracks I'd already made.

"So," hidden twigs snapped as we fumbled our way through with all of our merchandise, "is *now* a good time to talk about why you're being so weird lately and not chasing after all the pretty boys with me?"

"It's really not a big deal. Can we just not?"

"Excuse me, it *is* a big deal when I don't have my wing man. C'mon, Issy, it's *me*," Candice insisted, laying one hand over her heart, "you can tell me. No judgement. Is it a yeast infection? Syphilis?"

"Syphilis, Cee? *Really*?"

"Hey, I saw that drummer you left with the night of Tina's bachelorette party."

I shook my head in defeat, sighing, "*okay*." My tongue darted out to wet my suddenly dry lips, "the *actual reason* it's been a while," I had to stop and clear my equally dry throat, "is that it's all just been getting, *shit*, I don't know. *Boring.*"

When I lifted my eyes to continue, Candice was already laughing. She was full-on doubled over and clutching at her sides.

"Hey!" If I could've picked up a pinecone just then, I'd have chucked it at her face, "you said no judgment! Why're you even laughing?"

"I'm *not*, I'm not judging," she promised, "I'm laughing because I did *not* expect you to say that. Let's go out tonight - to the Paper Rooster. I'll get you laid."

I frowned, "are you listening? It's not that I don't think I can get laid," I told her, "it's like, every guy I meet and hook up with is the *same* and it's becoming such a waste of time. Does that make sense? What I want is something *different*."

"Different how?" Candice wiggled her eyebrows suggestively, "like, kinky?"

"I don't know, maybe."

"*Ooh*," she clucked happily, "my girl wants to get *spanked*." A broad grin tilted her lips, "I approve."

I scowled over my shoulder at her, "what? *No.*"

"Temperature play?"

I sighed, pressing my face into my hands, "I don't even know what that is."

She *tsked* at me, "no wonder you're bored! Dearest friend, you need to get online and do your research. I'm sure you'll find something that *tickles* your fancy."

"Can we just keep walking, please? All this shit is starting to get heavy."

"Hey, just trying to help. You're the one that brought it up."

I paused to frown at her again, "no, *I didn't.*"

She passed me without saying anything else, striding purposefully toward the clearing that marked the halfway point between the East side of town and our home. "Look," she was still stumbling toward the snow-covered meadow, "someone built something last night."

As I got closer, I could see that she was right. In the middle of the clearing was a snowman. Not just *any* snowman, though. Someone extremely artistic, and maybe just as horny as I was, had taken the time to carve out a jawline that could cut diamonds and some impressive-looking muscles for this snowman.

Damn.

The fact that he was at least six feet tall had Candice and I tilting our heads back and grinning up at the snowy masterpiece.

"*Hey, now,*" Candice hummed low, lips lifting in a mischievous smile, "here's a man for you, Issy."

I gave a quick bark of laughter, "give me another day and I might just be desperate enough."

"Hear that, Iceman? My friend Isobel might need to borrow your carrot for a little bit."

"C'mon, Cee, *gross*."

"And whattaya know," she turned to wink at me over her shoulder, "*temperature play*."

I still didn't understand what the hell she was babbling about.

"Too bad they put shorts on him," Candice pouted, pointing to Iceman's boxer shorts, which were also splendidly carved out of snow and ice.

"Yeah," I chuckled, "might be nice to see what's under them, huh?"

Candice's nose crinkled with her question, "think he's circumcised?"

"Candice," I said slowly, "something is *very* wrong with you."

"Wrong with *me*? You just said you'd fuck a snowman. Seriously, how long has it been?"

"Too damn long," I sighed. A dull ache began to settle between my thighs, reminding me again how hard up I truly was.

"Just think, an ice cock? No half-hard bullshit there."

"*Oh, my fucking god.*"

"Shit," Candice was digging through her heap of bags, oblivious to my disgust with her, "I think I dropped that scarf I got for my mom," she was already retracing her steps, "I'll be right back," she called.

I waited, glancing around the meadow and marveling at all its winter beauty. The bare branches of the trees were coated in ice so that when the Sun poked through the clouds, they glittered like exotic jewels. The wind picked up then, shaking the shimmering trees and whipping snow across the field.

Suddenly, something pitch black tumbled out of the forest and landed near my feet. I crouched to pick it up, turning in over in my hands.

"Is that a *top hat*?" Candice reappeared beside me, her mom's scarf being safely tucked back into a shopping bag.

"I just found it," I hitched a thumb over my shoulder, "it flew out of the trees." I ran the brim between my fingers, admiring the stiff fabric.

"You should put it on your snowman's head. Maybe he'll come to life," she teased.

I laughed along with her, but some tiny part of me wondered if maybe sexy Christmas miracles might just happen once in awhile?

We moved on from the clearing, finishing the hardest part of the hike, which was the steep hill just below the edge of our parking lot.

I'd nonchalantly tucked the mysterious top hat into one of my bags, some sixth-sense telling me to hang onto it.

"Well," Candice was digging her keys out of her coat pocket, "I'll see you tomorrow, right? For breakfast?"

I nodded, "yeah, is nine okay?"

"Sounds good to me."

"Cool, well, thanks for coming out with me today."

She just smiled, "now go do your research."

I frowned, "my...? Oh! Yeah, okay," I laughed, "maybe I will."

Finally comfortable in a pair of yoga pants, I settled myself in front of my desktop with yet *another* piping mug of cider.

Email, check. Credit card payment, check. What's next?

My fingers danced along the keys - *temperature play*. The search engine turned up - *wow* - okay, a lot of stuff, actually.

I read aloud to myself, "...hot or cold objects and substances used to stimulate the skin and create a sensual reaction...."

So, *hypothetically*, if I were to fuck a snowman with an ice dick, it seemed like it would be a pretty good time.

"*Girl*," I yawned, "just watch some porn and go to bed." A second yawn had me stretching my aching arms over my head. "Or maybe just go to bed."

Hitting off the lights as I went, my mind wandered briefly to what Candice had said about putting the hat on the snowman.

C'mon, Issy, I scolded myself, *that's just an old urban legend. It's not like that would actually work.*

I tried to push the irritating thoughts away with some really loud music pulsing through my headphones.

It's just a legend.

Once the moon had risen up over our apartment building, I crept quietly down the hallway to the service elevator. With all the thoughts of sugarplums and sexy snowmen dancing
in my head, I knew I'd never get any damn sleep unless I tried out Candice's idea, as crazy as it all sounded. I had the tattered hat gripped firmly in my hands, afraid the wind would try and take it back once I stepped outside.

The silence was almost deafening as I carefully made my way to the beginning of the trail. My boots crunched through the ice-topped snow and somewhere above me, one lonely owl called out to the sliver of shining moon.

A short trek later, the sexy snowman came into view, still sitting magnificently in the center of the clearing.

"This is so stupid," I muttered to myself, "*you're* so stupid." And yet, I kept moving toward him.

Next to Iceman again, the wind started to howl through the treetops, some strange melody whispering along my cheeks. Something like intuition tugged at my belly again.

Just put the damn hat on him. What's it gonna hurt to just try?

I held my breath and slowly lifted up the hat, placing it firmly on Iceman's head.

The clearing exploded with blistering gusts that raged across the open space, whipping my hair into my eyes. I coughed, battling against the sudden December storm.

When I managed to pull the hair free from my face, I was stunned to see two azure eyes sparkling down at me.

"*Holy*," I squeaked, "holy *fuck*. That actually worked. *You're actually alive*."

Iceman smiled, his straight, white teeth flashing like a beacon in the darkness. "Hi, Isobel."

My entire body felt frozen but I wasn't sure that it was from being outside. "Y-you know my name," I blinked.

"Earlier," the gravel of his voice brushed along my skin, raising goosebumps, "you were out here with your friend."

"And you could h-hear us talking?"

He nodded, a roguish smirk spreading across his full lips. "Yeah, I heard pretty much everything."

Embarrassment climbed up my neck and was probably settling in a red flush across my cheeks. It didn't help that Iceman was still wearing *only* boxer shorts, which had been transformed from snow into crimson satin. It took everything in me not to simply stare at his chest; at his amazingly lickable abs.

"Wow, okay, I have to be dreaming," my fingers twisted in my hair, like the prickling pain of it could somehow tug me back into waking. "This is just a weird sex dream," I heard myself whimper. "*Dammit*, this is Candice's fault."

"Isobel," his snowy hand was reaching for my chin, trying to get me to meet his eyes, "it's okay."

"How is this *okay*? Nothing about this is *okay*," I ranted. "I'm *talking* to a *snowman*. I need to *wake up* before things get weird." I frowned, "well, weird-*er*."

He cocked an eyebrow, "weirder?"

"Yeah, I mean," I couldn't look at anything but my boots just then, "earlier. The stuff we were saying. I was obviously *joking*."

"Got it," I could hear the smile in his words, "you don't actually wanna see what's under my shorts."

There was no suppressing the amused grin that came to my lips. Hadn't I just been telling Candice that I wanted something different? Well, it didn't get much different than *this*. I mean, yeah, it was beyond bizarre, but it was by no means a *nightmare*.

Ahh, what the hell. This definitely won't be boring, right?

It all might've been just a dream, but I could at least try to make it a good one. And if it *wasn't* a dream, well, I'd have to deal with that possibility in the morning.

I finally managed to lift my gaze to Iceman's. "What if I said that I actually *do*?"

His blue eyes lit up at my confession and he took a tentative step toward me, his hands reaching out to capture my waist. "This can be whatever you want," he started, "we don't have to," and then he trailed off, attempting to find the right words, "I mean, I *want* to. If you do," he grinned.

He was gazing down at me, just waiting patiently while my brain tried to catch up to the whole *situation*. Cold hands rested lightly on my hips, not pulling or grabbing, just *holding*.

This is different, I thought. And then, *wow, Isobel, that's really sad.*

I stared back up at him, trembling in the dark. Was I nervous or excited? What would this encounter be like? There was only one way to find out, really.

Leaning up on my tiptoes, I pressed my lips to his. They were *soft*, and a small chill ran down to my toes.

His lips plucked at mine, tongue darting out to beg entry into my mouth. There was that first slick slide and I heard someone moan.

Yeah, that was probably me.

Iceman's arms wound around my waist, hauling me against the hard line of his body.

"Wait," I gasped between kisses, "won't you melt?"

"Just a little," he panted, "it'll be worth it."

In the darkness of the forest, it was just me and Iceman, our hot breath misting out in front of our faces and spiraling toward the stars.

Sometime between that first electric kiss and the moment Iceman led me toward the edge of the clearing, nearer the trees, he'd managed to unzip my coat and push it off my shoulders.

I realized he was still only wearing boxers, now tented with his obvious arousal. But *me*, I had way too many layers on. I began to tug at the bottom of my shirt, forcing it over my head, and letting it drop to the ground beside us.

His frosty hands deftly unclasped my bra and it joined a growing pile of garments in the snow.

Iceman's mouth returned to mine. He sucked my lower lip between his teeth, humming with pleasure as my desperate body writhed against his. Soft hands found my breasts, the piercing cold turning my nipples into hard pebbles, begging for more of his attention. He rolled each pert bud between his fingers, the ecstasy of it all spearing directly to my throbbing clit until I didn't know how much more I could take.

His frozen hand traveled down the smooth planes of my belly, toward the hem of my yoga pants, and I nearly sobbed with relief. Finally, he was going to touch me where I needed him most.

One finger teased at the edge of my pants, "can I?"

I was having a hard time remembering what words were so I gripped his wrist and forced his hand down beneath the thin material.

I jolted against him, the cold sting of his digits forcing more blood to rush to my aching cunt. Now I knew what Candice and the online forums had been talking about.

"*Hhnnngg*," I groaned, my hips swiveling as I tried to fuck myself against his fingers, "*yes*."

He continued to tease along my wet slit, sliding his fingers around my entrance before returning to rub at my most sensitive bundle of nerves.

Yeah, I really couldn't take the teasing anymore. I needed him inside me. "Boxers," I mumbled, reaching for his waistband and pulling them down. I watched in awe as his hard cock sprung free of the material to rest against his lower belly.

After that, it was an excited frenzy of tearing my pants and panties off, not even caring if the storm happened to blow them away. In that moment, all I could think about was how much I needed Iceman to touch me.

Once again, his icy hands were on my heated skin, cupping my ass and lifting me up while I wrapped my thighs around his hips. My back found the rough bark of one of the pine trees, the scratch of it against my sensitive skin only fueling my pleasure.

His forehead touched mine and he drew a ragged breath, "are you sure?"

"*Dude*," I panted, absolutely mindless with arousal, "if you stop, I'm going to bring a blowtorch out here and-"

He pitched his hips forward and I couldn't keep the startled gasp from raking its way out of my throat. I wish my first thought had been, *oh, god, yes*, but it was more, *oh, god, fucking cold*.

There was no going back now. I'd officially been penetrated by a snowman. Was I going to tell

Candice about this? Would she even believe me? Wouldn't she wanna know that he *was* indeed circumcised? I guess there was still that possibility that this was all just an incredibly wet dream.

Why the fuck am I even thinking about Candice right now?

"Please," I heard myself whimper. And he knew – *just fucking knew* – what I was asking for. His hips pistoned faster, the solid *smack* a flesh hitting ice echoing through the dark branches above us.

This, I thought, *this is what I was looking for*.

The delicious, stinging stretch of him inside me was driving me *crazy*. His impossibly hard ice cock was hitting places no human man ever had before. Places that I didn't even know I *had*.

So close, so damn close.

Every smooth stroke of him inside me brought me so much closer to coming. Any second, that string inside my belly was going to snap and send me soaring into bliss. One more hard thrust and he hit, *oh my god, just the right spot*, and my entire world exploded into brilliant, dancing lights.

I couldn't even *breathe* and my mouth hung open in a soundless cry as he continued to pump in and out, working me through my high.

I came down slowly, shakily,and felt his lips against my hair, soothing my trembling body.

"*Holy shit*," was the only thing I could say.

The sound he made was somewhere between a chuckle and a groan.

As my breathing settled down, he began to move again, brows slanted with his concentration. The solid cold of his cock slammed in and out of the slick heat of me.

Minutes later, his hips began to stutter, his rhythm all but lost as he neared his end. Frigid hands gripped my body tighter and his face sank against the crook of my neck, tilting the top hat that was still somehow on his head.

"*Isobel*," he groaned a warning and came, cold bursts of icy water erupting inside me. He pulled out slowly, lowering me to the ground and steadying me against the tree.

It had all been so amazing, *he* was amazing, but almost instantly came the thought, *what happens when all the snow melts?* Already I didn't want to give him up.

He must have sensed the shift in my mood. A moment later, I felt his hands cupping my chin again.

"What is it?"

"I almost wish this wasn't a dream," I whispered back.

He smiled sadly but winked down at me, "don't worry, Isobel, I'll be back again next year."

The storm chose *that moment*, when we staring into each other's eyes, to snatch back the old top hat. I tried to grab it, but it flew above the tree branches and off into the forest.

When I turned back to Iceman, his blue eyes were just lumps of coal again, and *magically* his shorts were back, completely made out of snow once more.

"Bye, Iceman," I sniffed. I gathered up all my discarded clothes and dressed as quickly as I could. Without Iceman's touch, I was starting to freeze out there in the woods.

Morning dawned unseasonably warm, and buttery sunlight filtered through my curtains, hitting me in the face. With a tired groan, I remembered that I had to get ready for breakfast with Candice.

I met her in our lobby one minute past nine. She was already there, tapping her foot impatiently against the tile.

"Hey, loser, you're late," Candice moved toward me, "and you have a stick in your hair," she was already plucking it out and studying the foliage with a frown. "Were you out jogging through the woods this morning or something?"

My *dream* came flooding back. Along with the insane knowledge that *holy crap it totally wasn't a dream.* I smiled, "or something."

"Whatever," she looped her arm through mine, "let's go, I'm starving."

On our way through the parking lot, I peered into the trees and hoped that Iceman had been right. Maybe he'd be back again the next time it snowed, along with that magic top hat.

ADDISON KANE is an
independently published erotic romance
author from Philadelphia.

She can be reached by email at
addisonkaneauthor@gmail.com

Manufactured by Amazon.ca
Bolton, ON

15675890R00018